The World of
Jacky Blue
and Other Cats

The time has come
to tell my story – **Jacky's story**.
It's a long one, and I can't fit all my
adventures here... but I'll give you
just a little taste of what it's like to be
a cat and
a special one, too.

My name is **Jacky Blue** and
I live with my brothers, my mother
and an alley cat and two dogs and a bird,
and a family of humans
in a house in the woods...

Mother says we Blues are
very well-bred, pure Tonkinese –
a blend of Siamese and Burmese –
our **Dad** is Mr. Blue,
a sire of distinction – but he
doesn't live here. My mother's name is
Kit and my brothers
are **Tom** and **Rare**...

Story Link®
Program

Here we are

all lined up looking at something outside (probably a dog). That's **Mother** on the left – she's always got her bustle on. Of course, **Rare** is next to her – she worships him; he's her favorite because he most closely resembles Dad. While the rest of us have the customary Siamese blue eyes and brown points (paws, tail, ears and nose),

Rare's eyes are "aquamarine" and his points are "mauve".

Mother thinks
he's the most
beautiful thing
that ever happened –

Rare thinks so, too.

Tom's next to Rare –
he's the beefy
one.

He looks a little like an
old "Tom" dressed in a Siamese cat suit.
To tease him I often
ask him where the zipper is
on his coat.

Then there's me.

Rare might be
the most beautiful
and Tom
the biggest and
the strongest, but
I am
without argument
the smartest.

I also have
the most colorful
personality
and the most
to say.

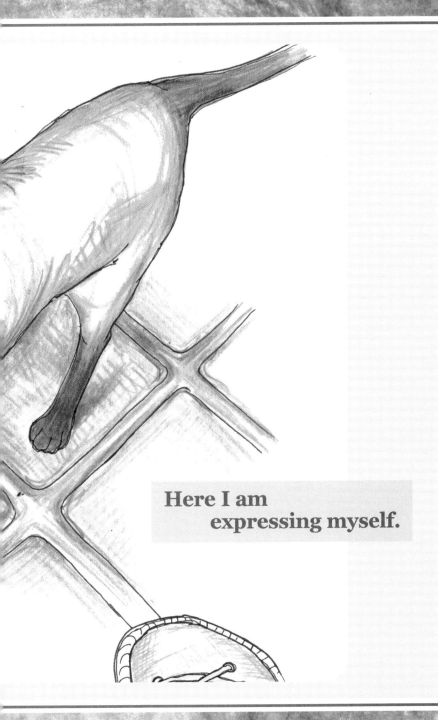

Here I am
    expressing myself.

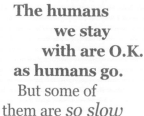

**The humans
we stay
with are O.K.
as humans go.**
But some of
them are *so slow*
to learn.
It's tedious work
training a human
to care
properly for the
needs of a cat.

For example,
we cats are
particular about our
toilet habits.
No cat likes to go
in a soiled pan.

If our pan is
repulsive
we might
go NEXT to it
or somewhere
AROUND it.

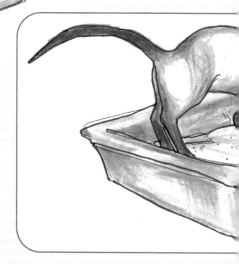

So, the moral is:
don't make such a
fuss if we dig to
China
and scatter
some litter
around
the litter box –
<u>and</u> make
sure our pans
are clean.

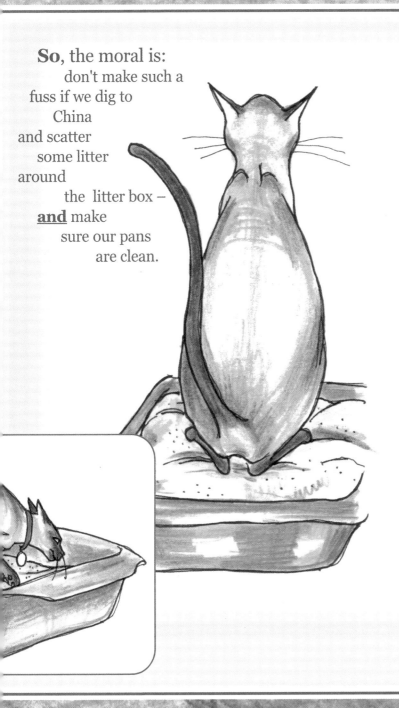

I have
many talents.

My human Mom
says,
*"Jacky, no one
can smile like
you do."*

And have you
ever heard of the term
"cat burglar"? There is no
door made that I can't go
in and out of at will.

If I have a
hankering
to go outside
**I just
do**,

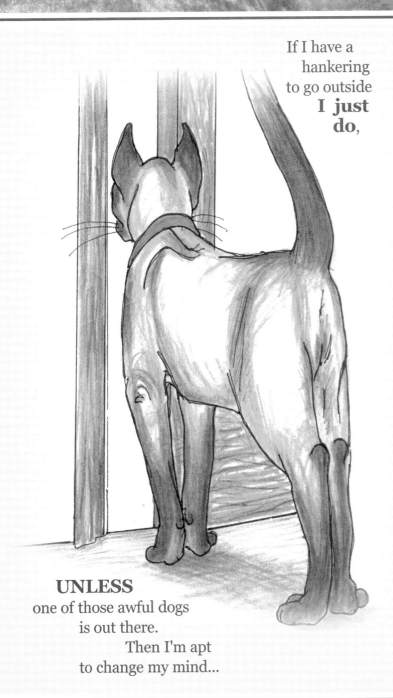

UNLESS
one of those awful dogs
is out there.
Then I'm apt
to change my mind...

But if I do go out, I often
come back in my favorite way:
through the deck window!

It's a cinch. Who said
a cat can't hang glide?

Sometimes when Tom and I play
we get a little rough and it turns
into a free-for-all.

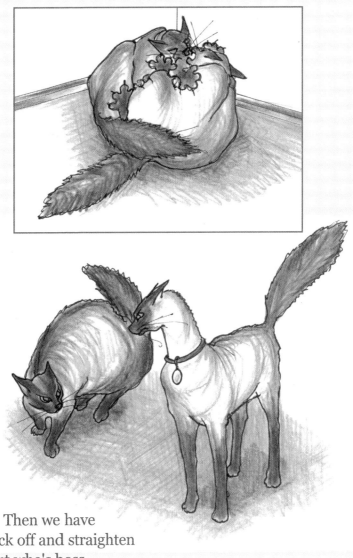

Then we have
to back off and straighten
out who's boss.

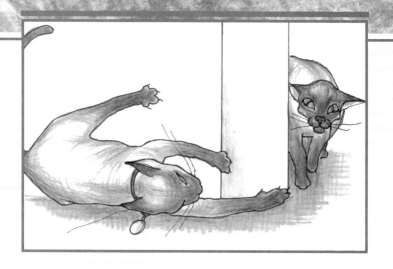

Occasionally, Ma tries to play. But she just can't,
and it's kind of pitiful. She's so cross-eyed she
just can't find me.

"Oh, Jack!" she cries.

"Where are you?"

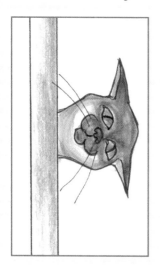

But mostly
we all get along fine
and frequently gather for a family washdown.
That's Mother working on Rare,
and Tom is grooming me...

However, there is another,
unrelated feline
who resides here –
a common housecat
named
Girly Rune Tijous,
who has the breeding
of a peasant
and the disposition of a
Halloween witch...

She is the basement mouser, and while we Blues are
secured in a bedroom for the night,
she comes upstairs
and prowls
the house.

**I like to spy
on her** from the
front deck
in the
daytime...

...I even shimmy down
            the post when I really want to give her
a piece of my mind –

        from my side of the closed (and locked)
basement door, of course...

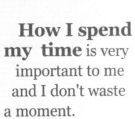

**How I spend
my time** is very
important to me
and I don't waste
a moment.
First, I have
a thing about baskets...
especially my basket
on top of the
refrigerator.

When it's cold outside

that spot always stays warm...
And, since it's in the room with the most
human activity, I can rest
cozy and well-assured I won't miss
a thing that goes on...

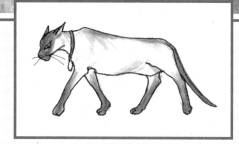

**When
I'm unhappy**
or really riled
about
something, I can stalk
to my basket, sit up in it
face-to-the-wall,
**and sulk
to my
heart's content...**

Suddenly, everybody wants to know:
"Jacky, what's wrong?"

Usually, I pout
because of something
stupid one of our humans
has done. One time
the Mom of the family
started
feeding us from little,
plastic margarine
containers.

I guess she thought
she was recycling —
we called it just being cheap.

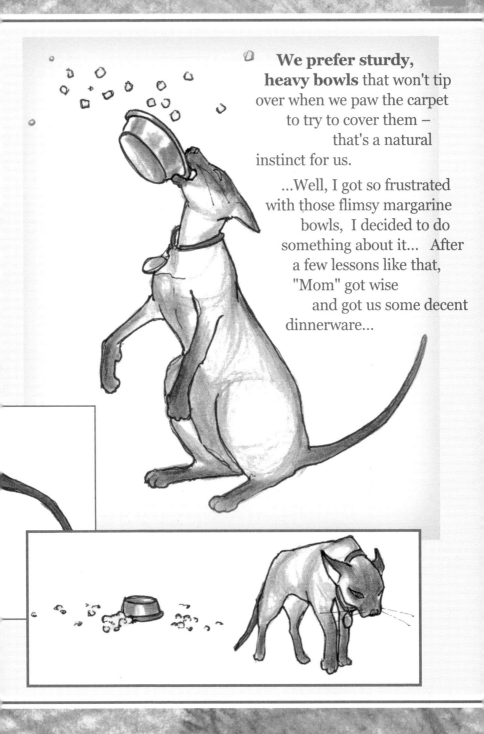

We prefer sturdy, heavy bowls that won't tip over when we paw the carpet to try to cover them – that's a natural instinct for us.

...Well, I got so frustrated with those flimsy margarine bowls, I decided to do something about it... After a few lessons like that, "Mom" got wise and got us some decent dinnerware...

I challenged her even further
with a fun little game I developed for cleaning days....
  Ever play **"chicken"** with the vacuum sweeper?

Tucked away
    in the hall,
I wait as the sweeper
    is prepared for use...

Click! It's on –
    now I hunker down, ready to spring
  as the dangerous thing approaches...

Z-O-O-O-M!!
I bolt across the hall just as the electric
monster grazes my nose (or toes)

and I startle the living daylights
out of "Mom"...**Great fun!**

I realize, though, that to live here
I have responsibilities, too. So, every weekday morning
during the school year,
I get up with the first human riser. I position myself
by plan so all the humans can hear me, and I
yell at them and call them names for the better part
of an hour, until they're all
thoroughly awake and on their way
to school or work...

For my efforts,
I get a lot of complaints:
**"Will someone please
shut that cat up??"**

...and even some out-and-out threats on my life:
"Jacky, I'm going *to brain* you if you don't be quiet!!"

...But someone's got to do it...

After everyone's gone, I hustle upstairs and settle in on an unmade bed for some much-needed rest and relaxation...

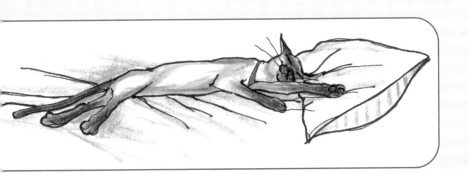

At a time like this,
I might indulge

in a leisurely bath...

Then I amble back downstairs
to enjoy some of my choice pastimes...
**That's me behind
the hearth...**

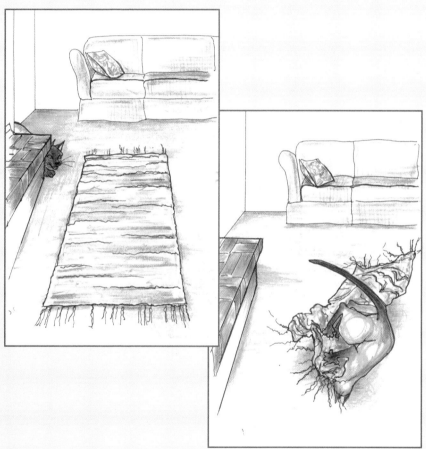

I just love it when that rug
is so carefully laid out, *smooth
and straight...*

In the kitchen,
I might give
the broom a chew,
though this is a practice
I mostly reserve
as a message
to our humans that our
food bowl is empty...

it's sort of boring when
no one is there
to see and scold...

See how my skill for thievery pays off...

I have a passion for graham crackers, and I
learned early on where they were kept.
My humans are so trained they
leave an open package for me
on the shelf in the cupboard...

Sometimes it's fun

to just fly around the house acting like a predator,
even if there's nothing really there...
Ma gets upset when I go wild...
She says, *"Oh, Jack! Why can't
you be more genteel **like your brother
Rare?"***

Well, the busiest thing
Rare does is

drape himself over the
bathroom towel bar and gaze
at his reflection in the mirror...
Pretty face, but oh,
what an empty head...

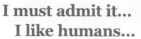

**I must admit it...
I like humans...**
I like to get in their faces
and read their eyes...
And they can get my
purr machine working better
than anything else...
My favorite human is Scott,
one of the
teenaged boys here...I sleep
on his bed
(when I'm not in one
of my baskets)...

He goes
away to school now,
so I have to show him

how much love
I've stored up
for him
every time he
comes home....

There's another human I like,
but he's young, inexperienced

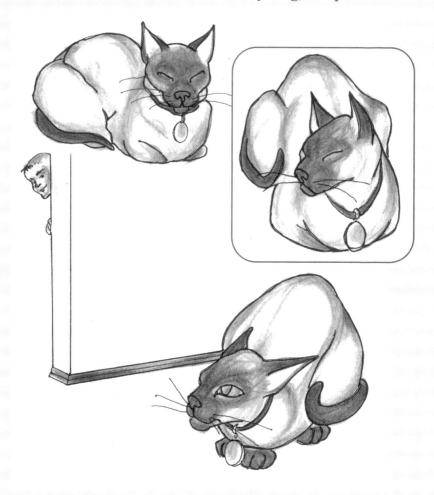

and not through with his training yet...
He stakes me out when
I'm totally relaxed –
doing "slipper" maybe...

I hear something! **Aha!**
Greg's stealthy footfalls
approaching...
Thinking he's caught me
completely offguard,
he tackles me
like a
football,
and –

always
careful

not to
hurt me –

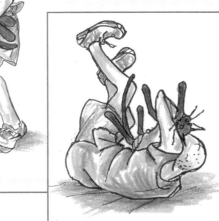

he rolls me over and makes up to me
like nothing
happened....**Crazy!**

Too, there's that younger,
      headstrong human named **Thad**
   who still thinks cats are toys...

he refuses to hold us how we like...

Happy for me,
he far prefers the company
of my brother Tom....

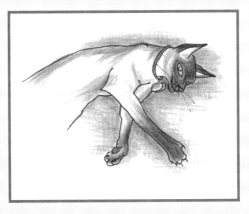

with their beefy builds
and husky appetites those two suit
each other pur-r-r-rfectly!

Speaking of Tom –
he and Rare once got into a litterpan
of trouble with Greg.

Greg
received a very attractive rabbit's foot
as a gift... he decided to keep it in his
room, where we Blues eat, sleep, etc...

Well, you already know about Rare's
limited thinking powers –
but Tom's even worse
when it comes to figuring things out...

Look at his tail.
It's permanently frozen in a question mark!
(And that's pretty much his state of mind
at any given time)...

Those two clowns sniffed out the rabbit's foot
and went overboard with it right away; they decided it
was prey and tried to kill it.

By chance, Greg caught them
and saved it just in time.

BUT, he tucked it under his plastic crocodile's pillow, satisfied it was
hidden from a cat (two cats!)...

When he came home from school, it was gone from the hiding place...
only to turn up later in our empty food bowl among a scattering of crumbs – **all chewed up with the fur completely gone...**

Some of us just can't manage that old hunting instinct...
Beasts!

You may wonder why
in some of my pictures I'm wearing a collar
and sometimes not... Collars are fine if they're loose
enough – but they can cause some problems...

After accidentally catching the "S" hook
on a blanket a few times I learned to yank my collar off
myself...

Thankfully, my humans
got tired of putting it back on...

...So, now life is just a little more serene
and more carefree...Here I am pretending
to bask in the rays of the Riviera...

and there I am on the deck rail thinking about
the wisdom of the ages and all the mysteries
of the universe...Life is good being a cat –
a special one, that is.